# Happy Birthday Lulu

To Albert
with love

You can also read
## Hello Lulu
ISBN 1 84121 728 X

and
## Lulu's Busy Day
ISBN 1 84121 590 2

ORCHARD BOOKS
96 Leonard Street, London EC2A 4XD
*Orchard Books Australia*
Unit 31/56 O'Riordan Street, Alexandria, NSW 2015
1 84121 735 2 (hardback)
1 84121 618 6 (paperback)
First published in Great Britain in 2000
First paperback publication in 2001
Copyright © Caroline Uff 2000
The right of Caroline Uff to be identified as the author
and the illustrator of this work has been asserted by her in
accordance with the Copyright, Designs and Patents Act, 1988.
A CIP catalogue record for this book is available from the British Library.
1 2 3 4 5 6 7 8 9 10 (hardback)
3 4 5 6 7 8 9 10 (paperback)
Printed in China

# Happy Birthday Lulu

## Caroline Uff

little 🌳 ORCHARD

This is Lulu.

Is it your birthday today, Lulu?

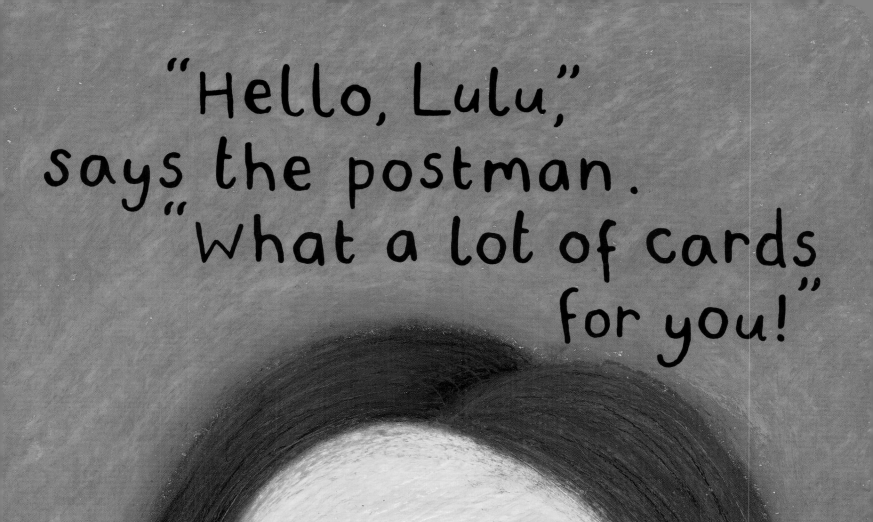

"Hello, Lulu",
says the postman.
"What a lot of cards
for you!"

At breakfast Lulu has a birthday hug

and
a big present.

# What's inside?

"Come and play with my new Noah's Ark," says Lulu.

The animals go in two by two.

Brring, brring!
Grandad rings up to wish
Lulu a very special day.

Lulu is busy cooking for her party. Mmm, that smells good.

Teddy has fun blowing up balloons. Puff, puff, puff.

Lulu helps lay the tea table.

It's time for Lulu to get dressed for her party.

Even Teddy has a
red ribbon to wear.
You look
beautiful,
Lulu.

Here come Lulu's friends.

"Thank you!" says Lulu as everyone gives her a present.

Dum dee dum, dee dum, dee dum!

# Lulu loves musical chairs.

Yum yum, it's teatime. Everyone sings,